Cat

Series "Fun Facts on Farm Animals for Kids"

Written by Michelle Hawkins

Cat

Series "Fun Facts on Farm Animals for Kids"

By: Michelle Hawkins

Version 1.1 ~July 2021

Published by Michelle Hawkins at KDP

Copyright ©2021 by Michelle Hawkins. All rights reserved.

No part of this publication may be reproduced, distributed or transmitted in any form or by any means including photocopying, recording or other electronic or mechanical methods or by any information storage or retrieval system without the prior written permission of the publishers, except in the case of very brief quotations embodied in critical reviews and certain other noncommercial uses permitted by copyright law.

All rights reserved, including the right of reproduction in whole or in part in any form.

All information in this book has been carefully researched and checked for factual accuracy. However, the author and publisher make no warranty, express or implied, that the information contained herein is appropriate for every individual, situation, or purpose and assume no responsibility for errors or omissions.

The reader assumes the risk and full responsibility for all actions. The author will not be held responsible for any loss or damage, whether consequential, incidental, special or otherwise, that may result from the information presented in this book.

All images are free for use or purchased from stock photo sites or royalty-free for commercial use. I have relied on my own observations as well as many different sources for this book, and I have done my best to check facts and give credit where it is due. In the event that any material is used without proper permission, please contact me so that the oversight can be corrected.

National Cat Day is October 29th.

The 1st breed of Cats was the Burmese and Siamese.

There are over 500 million Domestic Cats in the world.

Cats sweat through their paws.

There are over 94 million Cats in the world that people say are pets.

Cats are the 2nd most popular pet in the world.

Per the International Cat Association, there are 71 different breeds of Cats.

Having a Cat helps to relieve stress.

Cats have excellent hearing.

The average height of a Cat is nine inches.

Korat Cats are born with blue eyes that change to green.

Having a Cat can help people to avoid the risk of a heart attack.

Cats can not taste sweetness.

The 1st hairless Cat was the Sphynx.

Cats can run up to thirty miles per hour.

Cats are scared of cucumbers.

Manxes Cats are tailless.

Cats have twenty bones in their tail.

Cats have been around for over 12,000 years.

Cats can not see directly under their nose.

Cats have very flexible bodies.

The average age for an outdoor Cat is six years.

In certain parts of the world, it is illegal to declaw a Cat.

Cats can jump up to eight feet.

The most distinctive breed of Cats is the American Cat.

Cats have no eyelashes.

In a Cat's ear, there are twenty muscles.

The biggest Cat on record is forty-six pounds.

Most people have a Cat for companionship.

Male Cats are called Tom.

The average lifespan for an indoor Cat is twelve to eighteen years.

A Cat can smell 14 times stronger than a human.

Cats have 80 million scent receptors; humans have 5 million.

In 1963 a Cat was flown into space.

Longhaired Cats should be brushed at least once a day.

Cats can absorb shock when they land.

The majority of Ginger Cats are males.

Cats will use their tail for balance.

Cats can sense an earthquake before it happens.

Cats will sleep up to seventy percent of their time.

When a Cat licks you, they are marking their territory.

Cats will touch nose to nose to greet each other.

A Russian Blue Cat is gray but looks blue.

Dreaming about a white Cat is considered good luck.

A young Cat is called a Kitten.

Before the 1950's most cats lived outside.

The first year of a Cats life is equal to fifteen years of a human's life.

A Cats heart beats twice as fast as a human's.

Cats have three eyelids.

Cats have five toes on the front and four toes on the back.

The longest Cat recorded was 48 inches.

The average length of a Cat is sixteen to twenty inches.

The official Cat of the state of Maine is the Maine Coon Cat.

Cats can hear better than dogs.

Cats spend forty percent of their waking hours grooming themselves.

You can say hello to a Cat by blinking at them; if the Cat blinks back, they are happy.

Cats' teeth are suitable for hunting.

The claws on a Cat are continuously growing.

People are more likely allergic to Cats than dogs.

A female Cat is called a Molly or Queen.

The most popular Cat in the American Shorthair.

Cats can make over 100 different sounds.

An Ocicat Cat resembles a wildcat.

Cat Fancier Association says there are over 44 different Cat breeds.

There are 230 bones in a cat; humans have 206 bones.

Cats can move each ear separately.

The oldest Cat on record was thirty-eight years old.

Cats can rotate their ears 180°.

Cats are considered lethal hunters.

A Cat nose is like a fingerprint; each one is unique.

The smallest domestic Cat is the Singapura.

A Cat's rough tongue is used to clean itself.

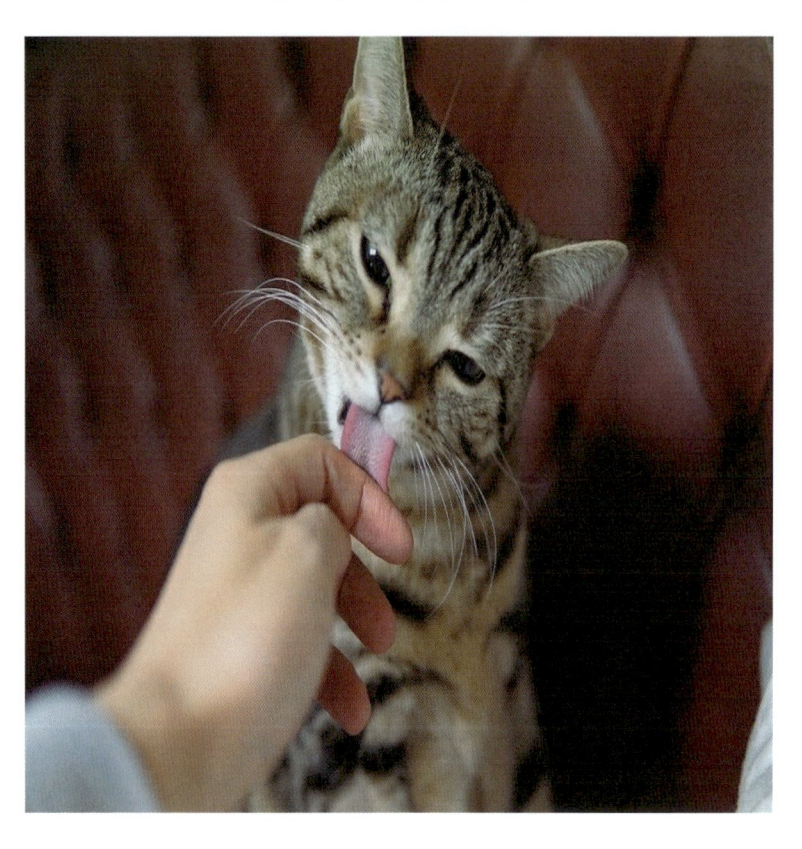

Cats meow to communicate with humans.

Most Cat households average two.

A group of adult Cats is called a Clowder.

Indoor Cats, on average live fifteen years.

Most Cats are lactose intolerant when they become adults and do not drink milk.

A Cat's pupil will dilate in the dark to see better.

In Ancient Egypt, Cats were considered sacred.

Cats have excellent vision at night.

Cats have a great sense of smell.

There are over 80 different colors of Persian Cats.

Six in ten households have at least one Cat.

Cats have a similar brain as humans do.

Europe used Cats for pest control.

Cats can hear five times better than a human can.

The scientific name for a Cat is Felis Catus.

Find me on Amazon at:

https://amzn.to/3oqoXoG

and on Facebook at:

https://bit.ly/3ovFJ5V

Other Books by Michelle Hawkins

Series

Fun Facts on Birds for Kids.

Fun Fact on Fruits and Vegetables

Fun Facts on Small Animals

Fun Facts on Dogs for Kids.

Fun Facts on Dates for Kids.

Fun Facts on Zoo Animals for Kids

Fun Facts on Farm Animals for Kids.